John Tenniel, Richard Doyle, John Leech

Benjamin Disraeli, Earl of Beaconsfield, K.G.

In Upwards of 100 Cartoons From the Collection of Mr. Punch

John Tenniel, Richard Doyle, John Leech

Benjamin Disraeli, Earl of Beaconsfield, K.G.
In Upwards of 100 Cartoons From the Collection of Mr. Punch

ISBN/EAN: 9783337166922

Printed in Europe, USA, Canada, Australia, Japan

Cover: Foto ©Raphael Reischuk / pixelio.de

More available books at **www.hansebooks.com**

THE

EARL OF BEACONSFIELD,

K. G.

CARTOONS FROM "PUNCH."

1843—1878.

Benjamin Disraeli.

EARL OF BEACONSFIELD,

K. G.

In Upwards of 100 Cartoons from the Collection of

"Mᴿ· PUNCH."

PUNCH OFFICE, 85, FLEET STREET, LONDON.

1878.

LONDON :
BRADBURY, AGNEW, & CO., PRINTERS, WHITEFRIARS.

Benjamin Disraeli.

Earl of Beaconsfield, K.G.

SON of Isaac D'Israeli, author of *Curiosities of Literature*, of Jewish extraction; born in London 21st December, 1805; published his political novel, *Vivian Grey*, 1825; travelled in the East between 1828 and 1831; contested Wycombe in 1831, and Marylebone, 1833, both unsuccessfully; was returned for Maidstone, 1837; for Shrewsbury, 1841; for Bucks, 1847; member of Sir R. Peel's party until Peel became a convert to Free Trade, from which time Mr. Disraeli allied himself closely with the Conservatives, of whom he became the leader in the House of Commons after the death of Lord George Bentinck in 1848; conspicuous for his attacks on Peel in Parliament; Chancellor of the Exchequer in Lord Derby's first Ministry, 1852; and in his second, 1858—9; in 1859 brought in a Reform Bill which was defeated by the Whigs; again Chancellor of the Exchequer in Lord Derby's third Ministry, July, 1866; brought in a second Reform Bill, based on Household Suffrage, which was passed, 1867; on Lord Derby's resignation, February, 1868, became Prime Minister, which office he resigned at the end of the year; on

Mr. Gladstone's Government resigning office, in consequence of their defeat on the Irish University Bill, March, 1873, Mr. Disraeli was commissioned by the Queen to form a Ministry, but declined to do so under the then circumstances. On Mr. Gladstone appealing to the country in 1874, the election returns placed him in a minority, and he resigned without meeting the new Parliament ; Mr. Disraeli succeeded him as Prime Minister and formed his cabinet, March, 1874 ; created Earl of Beaconsfield, August, 1876 ; first Plenipotentiary for Great Britain at the Congress of Berlin, 1878, and K.G. Lord Beaconsfield's principal novels (besides *Vivian Grey*) are *The Young Duke*, *Henrietta Temple*, and *Venetia*, and, since his entrance on political life, *Coningsby*, *Sybil*, *Tancred*, and *Lothair*.

London, 1878.

A LIST OF THE CARTOONS.

YOUNG GULLIVER AND THE BROBDINGNAG MINISTER.

☞ It was at this period that Mr. Disraeli commenced the attacks upon Sir Robert Peel, which were continued during the lifetime of that Statesman.—1845.

No. 1.

A POLITICAL APPLICATION OF AN
OLD FABLE.

☞ Mr. Disraeli's attacks upon Sir Robert Peel were at this time extremely splenetic and bitter.—1846.

THE RISING GENERATION—IN PARLIAMENT.

PEEL. *"Well, my little Man, what are you going to do this Session, eh?"*

D——LI (the Juvenile). *"Why—aw—aw—I've made arrangements—aw—to—smash —aw—Everybody."*

☞ At this time Sir Robert Peel had resigned the Conservative leadership in the House of Commons, which was assumed by Lord George Bentinck, assisted by Mr. Disraeli.—1847.

No. 3.

THE POLITICAL CHEAP-JACK.

"Now then, my Bucks,—let me have the pleasure of making you a few Presents,—
an assortment of valuable Pledges, warranted never to break," &c., &c.

☞ Mr. Disraeli was first returned for Buckinghamshire at the General Election in 1847.

No. 4.

THE PARLIAMENTARY TOOTS.

MRS. BLIMBER (DIS-R-LI). *"I think it convenient, TOOTS, to say to you, before the young gentlemen disperse, that you appear to me to have reached the lowwater mark of general contempt, and that there is not the least probability of your ever gaining another inch towards flood-tide again. All your friends are ashamed of you; all your enemies rejoice over you;* everybody is tired of you. In fact, TOOTS, you are, if I may express myself plainly, an unmitigated humbug, and a bore."

TOOTS (R-SS-LL) confused. *"It's of no consequence, thank you. It's all right. It's not of the least consequence in the world. Nothing is of any consequence, anywhere, I'm much obliged to you."*

☞ Mr. Disraeli, as one of the chiefs of the Opposition, severely criticised the conduct of Lord John Russell's Government.—1848.

No. 5.

COCK-A-DOODLE-DOO; OR, THE GREAT
PROTECTIONIST.

☞ Mr. Disraeli stood forth as the champion of the Agricultural Interest about this time.—1849.

No. 6.

THE FARMERS' WILL-O'-THE-WISP.

☞ Mr. Disraeli brought forward a resolution bearing upon Local Taxation, wherein the Agricultural Interest was subordinated to that of Real Property.—1849.

THE STATE OF THE NATION.

DISRAELI MEASURING THE BRITISH LION.

☞ Mr. Disraeli's motion for a Select Committee to consider the state of the nation, in consequence of the repeal of the Corn Law was rejected by a large majority.—1849.

No. 8.

THE PROTECTION "DODGE."

SUFFERING LANDHOLDER (in a solemn and sonorous tone, with a glance at the first-floor window).—"My kp—ind fer—iends, I am ash—amed to app—ear be—fore you, and to ex—pose my mis—er—able state. * * * "I am a lan—ded prop—er—i—etor re—duced to ger—eat mis—e—ry, ow—ing to the com—pe—tition of the foreigner. There is a ger—eat many of us as bad off as my—self, and the Count—er—y is o—being ruined all along of free—trade Sir Robert Peel and Mister Cob—den. We 'ave only twen—ty millions of money in the Bank, also an incr—ease of £38,235 on the Cust—oms, also £371,899 on the Ex—cise, and £44,560 on the In—come Tax, pity the poor Land—ow—ner," &c. &c.

☞ The hollowness of the "Protectionist" grievance was shown by the exceptionally prosperous state of the Exchequer at this time.—1850.

No. 9.

No. 10.

AGRICULTURE—THE REAL "UNPROTECTED FEMALE."

☞ Although the Free Trade policy had proved a real benefit to the country, the Agricultural districts had not as yet participated in it.—1850.

GULLIVER AND THE BROBDINGNAG FARMERS.

*" He called his hinds about him, and asked them (so I afterwards learned,) whether they had
ever seen in the fields any little creature resembling me ? "*—Vide "Gulliver's Travels."

☞ To compensate the Agricultural interests, Mr. Disraeli had moved to transfer £2,000,000 of Local
taxation to the Consolidated Fund. The motion was lost by a small majority.—1850.

DRESSING FOR A MASQUERADE.

MR. D—SR—LI AS A GREAT PROTECTIONIST LEADER.

☞ Mr. Disraeli, as the Farmers' Friend, made a motion in favour of the Relief of Agricultural Distress, which, however, was lost by a majority of 14.—1851.

THE GHOST OF PROTECTION APPEARING TO MR. DISRAELI.

☞ The Landowners and Farmers were still suffering from the repeal of the Corn Laws, and the efforts of Mr. Disraeli and the Conservative Party failed to procure from the Legislature any alleviation of their burdens.—1851. No. 13.

"THE GAME OF SPECULATION."

(AS PERFORMED AT THE THEATRE ROYAL, ST. STEPHEN'S.)

☞ Lord Derby became Premier this year, with Mr. Disraeli as Chancellor of the Exchequer and Leader of the House of Commons. The "Game of Speculation" was a popular drama.—1852.

No. 14.

THE PROTECTION GIANT.

" Fee, Fi, Fo, Fum ! | *Be he Alive, or be he Dead,*
I smell the Blood of an Englishman ; | *I'll grind his Bones to make my Bread."*

☞ The Conservative Party being now in Office, and their policy with regard to Free Trade being ambiguous, the Anti-Corn-Law League was revived at Manchester.—1852.

No. 15.

NEW CORN LAW !

UP GOES THE QUARTERN LOAF.

DERBY. *"Now, Gents, Give us only a Little Encouragement—Say a Five Shilling Duty—and 'UP' Goes the Quartern Loaf!"*

☞ In addressing the Electors of Buckinghamshire, Mr. Disraeli had intimated that the Government would be mindful of the Agricultural interests.—1852.

No. 16.

A PLAIN QUESTION.

MR. BULL. "*Now, Sir, don't let us have any more Derby Dilly Dallying. What are your Intentions towards Miss Britannia?*"

☞ At a meeting of the Liberal members called by Lord John Russell, it was resolved to press the Government for a declaration of its policy.—1852.

AN EASY PLACE.

THE JUDICIOUS BOTTLE-HOLDER. *"Well, Dizzy, how do you like your Place?"*
DI——I. *"O, Jolly! Capital Wages, and only got to Carry out these Light Things at present."*

☞ Mr. Disraeli, as Chancellor of the Exchequer, adopted generally the financial arrangements of the previous Government, on the plea that his Party were in a minority.—1852.

No. 18.

A BIT OF ANIMATED NATURE.

THE PROTECTIONIST CUCKOO IN THE HEDGE SPARROW'S NEST.

☞ The Militia Bill, which had proved fatal to the Whig Ministry, was carried by the Conservative Government by a large majority, and materially strengthened their position.—1852.

No. 19.

THE EASTER RECESS.

Dizzy. "Oh, no! I'm not at all Giddy. I should like to go ever so Much Higher."

☞ The dissolution of Parliament was postponed until the autumn, when the Government hoped to obtain a majority,—in which however they were disappointed.—1852.

No. 20.

THE "CALCULATING" BOY GETS THE PRIZE FOR ARITHMETIC.

☞ Mr. Disraeli produced his first Budget, which was favourably received.—1852.

THE DOWNING STREET CAD.

CONDUCTOR. *"Would any 'Party' go Out to oblige a Lady?"*

☞ The Conservative Party, when in power, made no effort for the relief of Agriculture,
or in the revival of Protection.—1852.

No. 22.

THE POLITICAL CHAMELEON.

☞ Mr. Disraeli and the Conservative Party were thought to be trimming towards Free Trade in anticipation of the General Election.—1852.

"A DISSOLVING VIEW."

☞ The result of the General Election was to leave the Conservative Party still in a minority. The triumph of Free Trade principles was complete.—1852.

SOMETHING "LOOMS IN THE FUTURE."

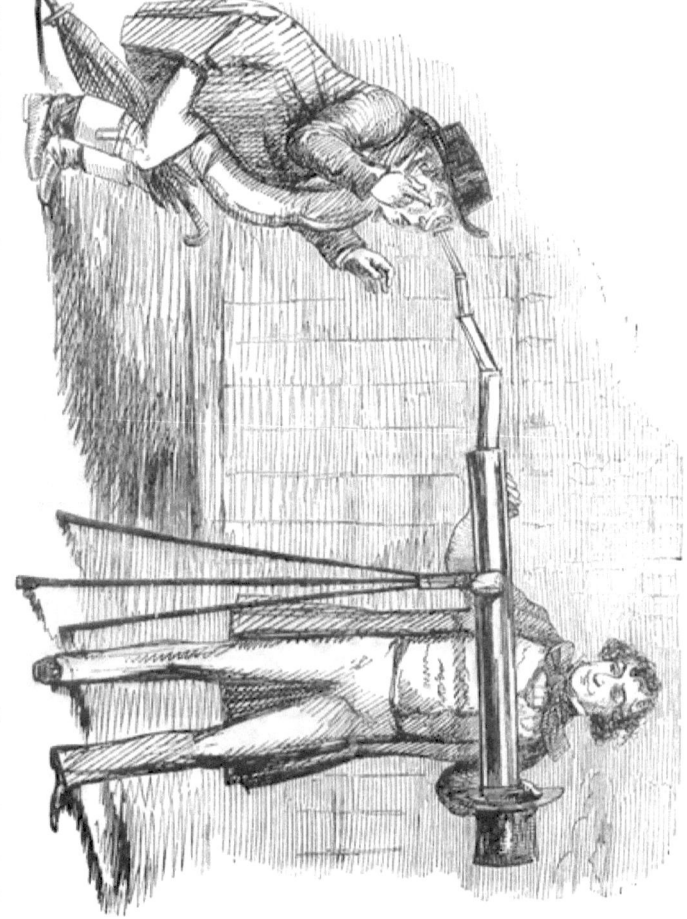

Mr. Disraeli, in his address to the Electors of Buckinghamshire, had declared that it was the intention of Her Majesty's Ministers to do something in the future for the Agricultural Interest.—1852.

No. 25.

A DIP IN THE FREE TRADE SEA.

" There, take off his Coat like a good little Ben, and come to his Cobden."

☞ The Leaders of the Conservative Party announced that they did not intend to return to the policy of Protection.—1852.

THE POLITICAL TOPSY.

" I 'spects nobody can't do nothin' with me !"—Vide "Uncle Tom's Cabin."

☞ The versatility and talent of Mr. Disraeli were sometimes of inconvenient service to his party.—1852.

MRS. GAMP TAKING THE LITTLE "PARTY SHE LOOKS AFTER BACK TO SCHOOL.

☞ Mrs. Gamp (the "Morning Herald," since defunct) was the special organ of Mr. Disraeli and the Protectionist Party.—1852.

A SCENE FROM ENGLISH HISTORY.

QUEEN ELEANOR AND FAIR ROSAMOND.

☞ The Free Trade Party, being in the majority in the new Parliament, left Mr. Disraeli with the only alternative.—1852.

No. 29.

A DIRTY TRICK—BESPATTERING DECENT PEOPLE.

☞ Mr. Disraeli, resenting the loss of office, was unsparing in his criticisms upon Lord Aberdeen's Coalition Ministry.—1853.

SWELL MOB at the OPENING OF PARLIAMENT.

Punch (A 1). "*Now then! What's your Little Game?*"

D—z—y. "*Our Little Game! Nothin'—We're only 'Waiting for a Party.'*"

☞ The Conservative Party were in hopes, at this time, of attracting to themselves the remnant of the "Peelites."—1857.

No. 31.

Dis—li.'.   G—as—L.

THE BALANCING BROTHERS OF WESTMINSTER.

Mr. Disraeli moved an amendment to the Budget of Sir G. Cornewall Lewis (then Chancellor of the Exchequer), in which he was supported by Mr. Gladstone.—1857.

No. 32.

THE ASIATIC MYSTERY.

☞ Mr. Disraeli moved for a Royal Commission to enquire into the grievances of the Natives which had
led to the mutiny in India.—1857.

No. 33.

PALMERSTON SELLING OFF.

☞ Lord Palmerston's Government was defeated on the 19th of February, and the Conservatives came into power.—1858.

THE RIVAL, BLACK DOLLS.

An "India Bill" had been introduced by Lord Palmerston as well as by Mr. Disraeli, neither of which was carried beyond the first reading.—1858.

DIZZY AND HIS CONSTITUENT.

☞ Mr. Disraeli had been addressing his Buckinghamshire constituents about this time.—1858.

No. 36.

THE LAST PANTOMIME OF THE SEASON.

☞ The Reform Bill introduced by Mr. Disraeli was rejected in the House of Commons by a majority of 39.—1859.

GREAT POACHING AFFRAY ON THE LIBERAL PRESERVES.

J—N R—SS—LL. *"Now then, you Sir! Give up that Gun!"*

☞ The defeat of the Government followed upon an amendment to their Reform Bill moved by
Lord John Russell.—1859.

THE ANGLERS' RETURN.

☞ On an appeal to the country, and the re-assembling of Parliament, the Government were found to be in a minority of 48.—1859.

A DERBY OBSTRUCTION.

Dizzy. "Shan't get out o' the way. I'd like to upset the lot of yer!"

☞ Mr. Disraeli, during a debate on the Budget, bitterly attacked Lord Palmerston's Ministry, declaring that they had "strained the Constitution."—1861.

A DERBY SPILL.

☞ Mr. Gladstone's Budget was accepted by the House of Commons, after several nights' debate, by a majority of 15.—1861.

No. 41.

THE FIGHT AT ST. STEPHEN'S ACADEMY.

MRS. GAMP. *"Never mind, my dear! you done yer werry best to win; which that*
Master Gladsting is such a huncommon strong boy!"

☞ Mr. Disraeli's Resolution condemning the policy of Earl Russell's Government towards Denmark
was defeated by a majority of 18.—1864.

No. 42.

DRESSING FOR AN OXFORD BAL MASQUÉ.

" The question is, is Man an Ape or an Angel? (A Laugh.) *Now, I am on the side
of the Angels.* (Cheers.)"—Mr. Disraeli's Oxford Speech, Friday, November 25.

☞ In addressing the Oxford Diocesan Society in a speech having reference to the policy of the Conservative
Party towards the Church, Mr. Disraeli made the above declaration, which gave rise to much comment.—1864.
No. 43.

DIZZY'S K'RECT CARD FOR THE "DERBY" (?)

"K'rect card, my noble Sportsmen!"—"K'rect Card!"—"Church in Danger!"—
"Lateral Reform!"—"K'rect Card!"

☞ In view of the approaching General Election, Mr. Disraeli, in an address to the Buckinghamshire electors, raised the cry of the Church in danger, and declared for a lateral extension of the franchise.—1868.

No. 44.

DIZZY'S ARITHMETIC.

PAM. "*Now, then, Youngster, you've no call to be a chalking that wall; and if you ɔ do a sum, you might as well do it right!*"

☞ The Conservative Party had hoped to gain additional strength at the General Election—but c contrary they lost 25 seats.—1865.

No. 45.

PUDDING BEFORE MEAT.

EARL GR—V—N—R. "*Why, John! Beef before Pudding!*"

DIZZY. "*Ha! Ha! What an absurd idea!*"

☞ On the introduction of Lord Russell's Reform Bill, Earl Grosvenor moved that it should not be discussed until the Government included their scheme for the re-distribution of seats.—1866.

No. 46.

THE FIRST QUESTION.

WORKING-MAN. "*Well, Gentlemen, what are* YOU *going to do for me?*"
LORD DERBY (aside to DIZZY). "*Ah! if he were only a Racehorse now——*"
DISRAELI. "*Or an Asian Mystery——*"

☞ Lord Derby had just formed his third Government, Mr. Disraeli being again Chancellor o
Exchequer. They declined to pledge themselves upon the Reform question.—1866.

No. 47.

POLITICAL "ECONOMY."

MANAGER. *"Now, then, Benjamin, what have we got for the Opening Scene?"*
PROPERTY-MAN. *"Well, sir, here's the old '59 Banner! A little touching up'll make it as good as new."*

☞ Numerous demonstrations in favour of Reform having taken place during the autumn, the Conservative Leaders were compelled to take up the question.—1866.

No. 48.

"HEADS I WIN, TAILS YOU LOSE."

" Sir, the meaning that we attribute to the words I have just read is, that, under the circumstances in which the House finds itself, it is in our opinion expedient that Parliamentary Reform should no longer be a question that should decide the fate of Ministries." (Loud laughter at this capital joke.)—Vide Speech of CHANCELLOR OF EXCHEQUER, Feb. 11, 1867.

☞ Mr. Disraeli introduced the Government proposals for Reform in a series of Resolutions, which were afterwards abandoned.—1867.

No. 49.

THE HONEST POTBOY.

DERBY (aside.) "*Don't froth it up this time, Ben. Good measure—the Inspectors have their eye on us.*"

☞ A majority of the Cabinet had agreed to introduce an extensive measure of Reform, which was followed by the resignation of General Peel, and Lords Carnarvon and Cranbourne.—1867.

No. 50.

BLIND MAN'S BUFF.

"*Turn round three times, and catch whom you may.*"

☞ The scheme of Mr. Disraeli's Reform Bill was largely altered by amendments in its passage through the House.—1867.

THE "IRREPRESSIBLE LODGER."

MRS. DIZZY (THE CHARWOMAN). "*Well, all I can say is—after the* EIGHTH OF APRIL *I dessay we may be able to accommodate the lot of yer.*"

☞ Mr. Disraeli agreed to include the Lodger Franchise in his Reform Bill, in Committee, which was fixed for April 8th. He declared himself the Father of the Lodger Franchise.—1867.

No. 52.

EXTREMES *MUST* MEET; OR, A BIT OF PRACTICAL SCIENCE.

PROF. D—R—I. "*But you see, to complete the circle, positive and negative* MUST *join hands.*"

☞ The principle of the Reform Bill was Household Suffrage qualified by payment of Rates, thus including all classes in the enjoyment of the Franchise.—1867.

No. 53.

THE DERBY, 1867. DIZZY WINS WITH "REFORM BILL."

MR. PUNCH. *"Don't be too sure; wait till he's* WEIGHED.*"*

☞ The first division on the Reform Bill in Committee resulted in a majority of 21 for the Government in a full House.—1867.

No. 54.

THE POLITICAL EGG-DANCE.

☞ Mr. Disraeli's dexterous management of the Reform Bill in Committee enabled him to defeat several amendments moved by the Opposition.—1867.

No. 55.

No. 56.

"THE RETURN FROM VICTORY."

(With Mr. Punch's apologies to Mr. Calderon, R.A.)

☞ Mr. Disraeli's Reform Bill was read a third time, and passed the House of Commons on July 15th, to the great rejoicing of the Conservative journals.—1867.

PUFF AT ST. STEPHEN'S.

FAGIN'S POLITICAL SCHOOL.

" Now, mark this; because these are things which you may not have heard in any speech which has been made in the city of Edinburgh. (Laughter and cheers.) I had—if it be not arrogant to use such a phrase—TO EDUCATE OUR PARTY. It is a large party, and requires its attention to be called to questions of this kind with some pressure. I had to prepare the mind of Parliament and the country on this question of Reform."—MR. DISRAELI's Speech at the Edinburgh Banquet.

☞ Mr. Disraeli had asserted that no Party could lay claim to a monopoly of Liberal principles—hence the Government were quite at liberty to deal with the Reform question.—1867.

THE NEW HEAD MASTER.

☞ On the resignation of Lord Derby Mr. Disraeli became Prime Minister, February 27th.—1868.

No. 59.

RIVAL STARS.

Mr. Bendizzy (Hamlet). "'*To be, or not to be, that is the question:*'—*Ahem!*"

Mr. Gladstone (out of an engagement). [Aside.] "'*Leading business,*' *forsooth! His line is* '*General Utility!*' *Is the Manager mad? But no matter-rr—a time* WILL *come——*"

☞ Though Mr. Disraeli was in office, his Party were in a minority in the House of Commons. The Opposition, under the nominal leadership of Mr. Gladstone, was disorganised.—1868.

No. 60.

STEERING UNDER DIFFICULTIES.

Ship's Captain. *"Give up the helm?—Resign the command?—Never! Come one, come all, I stick to my craft. Back, I say!—One step in-board, and I blow up the ship. Ha, ha!!"*

☞ Mr. Gladstone's Irish Church Suspensory Bill was carried against the Government by large majorities.—1868.

No. 61.

THE POLITICAL LEOTARD.

"It is a very old trick of mine," writes M. Leotard, "to make the belief to fall, and then to arrive on my feet."—Morning Paper.

☞ Instead of resigning after his defeat, Mr. Disraeli continued to hold office, promising a dissolution of Parliament in the autumn.—1868.

No. 62.

BEN AND HIS BOGEY.

MRS. BULL. *"I'll teach you to frighten people, Master Benjamin."*

☞ In his address to the Buckinghamshire electors, Mr. Disraeli endeavoured to alarm the country by declaring that the Church of Rome would be the only gainer by disestablishment.—1868.

No. 63.

RIVAL ACTORS.

(Mr. Gladstone, as William Tell, has been called before the curtain "amid the deafening plaudits of a House crammed to the ceiling.")

Mr. Bendizzy (Jeremy Diddler). *"He's got the House with him, that's certain.   Ahem! I must give 'em a touch of my* Art.*"*

☞ The general feeling throughout the country during the autumn was antagonistic to the Government.—1868.

No. 64.

A POLITICAL PARALLEL.

"See, where his Grace stands 'tween two clergymen!"—Vide RICHARD III., Act iii., Scene 7.

☞ The approaching General Election was to turn upon the Irish Church question, and the Government were assured of the full support of the Clergy.—1868.

No. 65.

"CRITICS."

(Who have not exactly "failed in literature and art.")—See Mr. D.'s New Work.

Mr. G-D-S-T-NE. *"Hm!—Flippant!"*   Mr. D-S-R-LI. *"Ha!—Prosy!"*

☞ Mr. Disraeli's latest novel, "Lothair," was published at this time, as was also Mr. Gladstone's work on Grecian Mythology.—1870.

No. 66.

THE STRONG GOVERNMENT.

Rex (*a rude boy*). "Now, then, all together!—and be very careful as you don't scrape yourselves!"

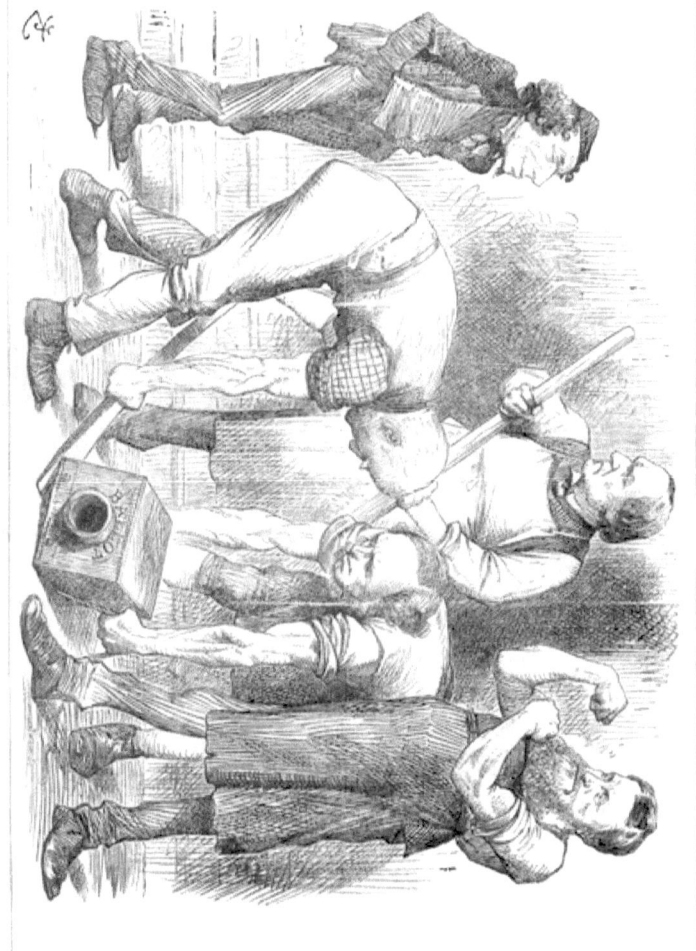

☞ The Ballot Bill was introduced by the Government towards the close of a busy Session, and was not altogether palatable to their supporters.—1871.

No 67.

"OUT OF THE BAG!"

DIZZY. "*Off! Of course he is! Ah, my dear Lord Butterfingers, you should leave this kind of delicate business to your* ACCOMPLISHED LEADER. *Ahem!!*"

☞ Overtures were made by certain members of the Upper House to the Trades Union Leaders—in supposed antagonism to Mr. Disraeli. The movement was a failure.—1871.

THE LANCASHIRE LIONS.

"So have I heard on inky Irwell's shore,
ANOTHER LION *give a louder roar,*
And the first lion thought the last a bore."—Bombastes Furioso.

☞ Mr. Disraeli received an enthusiastic welcome in Lancashire. In his speech at Manchester he likened the occupants of the Ministerial bench to a row of extinct volcanoes.—1872.

THE CONSERVATIVE PROGRAMME.

"Deputation below, Sir.—Want to know the Conservative Programme."

RT. HON. BEN. DIZ. *"Eh!—Oh!—Ah!—Yes!—Quite so! Tell them, my good Abercorn, with my compliments, that we propose to rely on the Sublime Instincts of an Ancient People!!"* [See Speech at Crystal Palace.

☞ A great Conservative demonstration was made at the Crystal Palace in recognition of the growing unpopularity of the Government. Mr. Disraeli refrained from committing his Party to a definite programme.—1872.

THE TWO AUGURS.

DISRALIUS. "*I always wonder, Brother, how we Chief Augurs can meet on the opening day without laughing!*"

GLADSTONIUS. "*I have never felt any temptation to the hilarity you suggest, Brother; and the remark savours of flippancy.*"

☞ Mr. Disraeli was more successful as a leader of his Party or of the House of Commons than his great antagonist.

PARADISE AND THE PERI.

" Joy, joy for ever ! My task is done—
The gates are passed, and Heaven is won !"—Lalla Rookh.

Mr. Disraeli had now for the first time a majority in Parliament. He became Prime Minister on the rejection of the Liberal Administration by the constituencies at the General Election.—1874.
No. 73.

THE WINNING "STROKE."

PUBLICAN. "'Ooray! Glad you've won, Sir."

DIZZY. "Thanks. I knew those SLIDING SEATS would upset 'em!"

☞ Some portion of the Conservative success was supposed to be due to the Publican interest, and to the operation of the Ballot.—1874.

No. 74.

THE GREAT "TRICK ACT."

RING-MASTER (MR. CROSS). *"Now, then, Mr. Wittler, stand out o' the way!"*

CLOWN (LITTLE WITTLER). *"Oh ah, of corse! Of corse I gave 'er a leg-up, and chalk'd 'er shoes of corse, and of corse I'm to get nothing for it! That's what I call Wittler's allowance!"* [EXIT, disgusted.

☞ The Intoxicating Liquors Bill passed by the Government created much disappointment to their supporters amongst the Licensed Victuallers.—1874.

No. 75.

A REAL CONSERVATIVE REVIVAL.

"*We have little or no FISH, Gentlemen; but at least we have revived that great and Conservative institution, THE MINISTERIAL FISH-DINNER!!!*"

☞ The number of measures passed by Mr. Disraeli's Government compared unfavourably with what had been done by the preceding Administration.—1874.

No. 76.

"GOOD-BYE!"

D—sr—li. *"Sorry to lose you!—I began with books; you're ending with them. Perhaps you're the wiser of the two."*

☞ Mr. Gladstone formally relinquished the Leadership of the Liberal Party, and made only an occasional appearance in Parliament during the Session.—1875.

No. 77.

THE INDIGNANT BYSTANDER.

MR. GLADSTONE. "*Don't you see, Sir, they're* DOING *you? You* MUST *lose!—Really, the Police ought to interfere!*"

DIZZY (a Simple Countryman!) "*Don't mind* HIM, *Sir! It's all his spite! He once kep' a table hisself!*"

☞ The Savings Banks Bill introduced by the Government was strongly opposed by Mr. Gladstone. The Bill was afterwards withdrawn.—1875.

No. 78.

MORE SLAVERIES THAN ONE.

RIGHT HON. B. D. "*Now that your Highness has seen the blessings of Freedom, I trust we may rely upon your strenuous help in putting down Slavery!*"

SULTAN SEYYID BARGHASH. "*Ah, yes! Certainly! But remember, O Sheikh Ben Dizzy,* CONSERVATIVE PARTY VERY STRONG *in Zanzibar!*"

☞ The Sultan of Zanzibar made a visit to Europe, and remained six weeks in London. He was pressed by the Government to use his influence to stop the Slave traffic in his dominions.—1875.

No. 79.

"PERMISSIVE" GOVERNMENT.

Lord H. *"After all's said and done, you exist only on sufferance, you know."*
Right Honourable D. *"'Sufferance,' my dear Hartington!—*
'Sufferance is the badge of all our tribe'!!!"
MERCHANT OF VENICE, Act i, Scene 3.

☞ Lord Hartington, as Leader of the Opposition, strongly animadverted on the feebleness of the Government and the comparative uselessness of their legislation.—1875.

No. 80.

"MOSÉ IN EGITTO!!!"

☞ Mr. Disraeli extorted the admiration of the country by purchasing for £4,000,000 on behalf of the Government the shares in the Suez Canal held by the Khedive of Egypt.—1875.

No. 81.

MYSTERIOUS CABINET

ROYAL COMMISSION

SECOND FUGITIVE SLAVE CIRCULAR

THE "EXTINGUISHER" TRICK.

"Here you perceive 'Fugitive Slave Circular' Number Two—Number One having disappeared already! I now take this Cone into my hand;—it resembles an Extinguisher, and is called a 'Royal Commission.' I place it over the 'Circular,' and—hey, presto!—on raising it again, 'Circular' Number Two WILL HAVE DISAPPEARED!"

☞ A Circular addressed by the Admiralty to the Commanders of H.M.'s Navy on the reception of Fugitive Slaves excited the disapproval of the country. The second was equally condemned. Mr. Disraeli evaded censure by referring the subject to a Royal Commission.—1876.

THE LION'S SHARE.

"*Gare à qui la touche!*"

☞ The acquisition of the Suez Canal Shares was accepted by the country as securing the safety of "The Key to India."—1876.

No. 83.

CIVIL SERVICE STORES.

"What can we do for you, Madam? Royal Commission?—Select Committee?—Papers?—
Careful Consideration?—Official Inquiry? Anything to oblige!"

☞ The Government were charged with the too-frequent practice of evading responsibility by referring
embarrassing subjects to a Royal Commission or a Select Committee.—1876.

No. 84.

"NEW CROWNS FOR OLD ONES!"

(ALADDIN *adapted.*)

☞ The Bill for adding to the Royal Titles that of Empress of India, though pressed forward by the Government, was scarcely approved by the country.—1876.

No. 85.

"THE JOLLY ANGLERS."

(A HOLIDAY IDYLL.)

BENJAMIN (to ST-FF-D N-THC-TE). "*Aha! Dear Boy! that's the sort o' Bait to catch the* 'HUNDRED-AND-FIFTY-POUNDERS!' *What sport we* SHALL *have!!!*"

☞ The main features in the Budget were the addition of a penny to the Income Tax and extending exemption to incomes of £150 per annum.—1876.

No. 86.

THE SPHINX IS SILENT.

☞ Servia and Montenegro having declared war against Turkey, and thus re-opened the Eastern Question, both Parliament and the country were anxious to know the policy of the Government, but Mr. Disraeli declined to yield information.—1876.

NEUTRALITY UNDER DIFFICULTIES.

Dizzy. "Bulgarian Atrocities! I can't find them in the 'Official Reports'!!!"

☞ The country was deeply stirred by the dreadful outrages in Bulgaria, and Mr. Disraeli's attitude of official indifference called forth wide disapprobation.—1876.

No. 88.

EMPRESS AND EARL;

OR, ONE GOOD TURN DESERVES ANOTHER.

LORD BEACONSFIELD. *"Thanks, your Majesty. I might have had it before! Now I think
I have EARNED it!"*

☞ Mr. Disraeli, at the close of the Session, was raised to the Peerage by the title of
Earl of Beaconsfield.—1876.

No. 89.

No. 90.

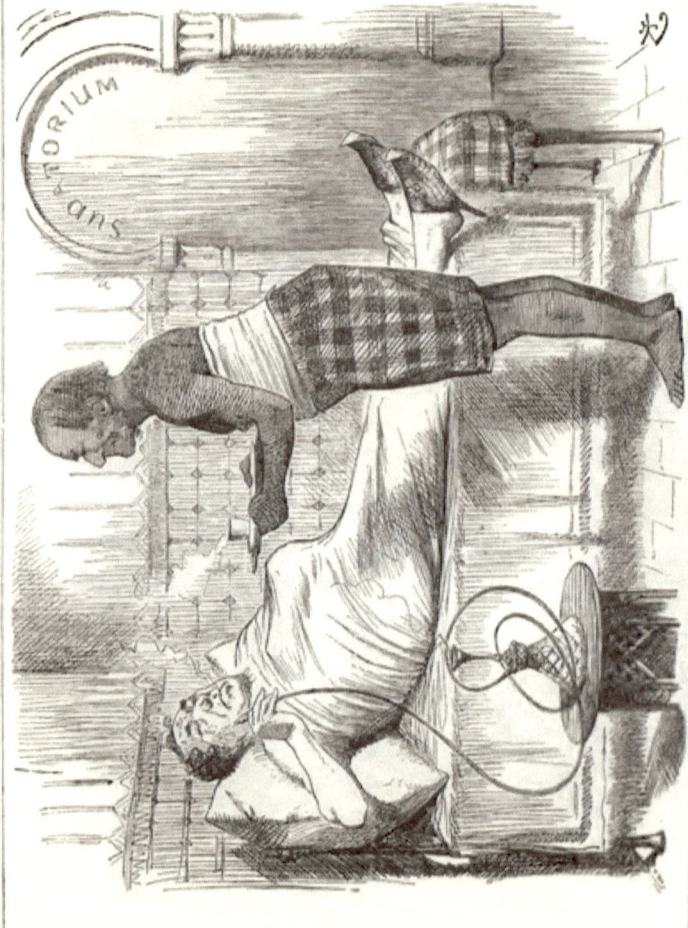

THE TURKISH BATH.

ATTENDANT. "*How do you feel after your bath, my lord?*"

LORD B. "*Pretty comfortable, thank you—(Aside. Lost some weight, I fancy.)—You made it so confoundedly hot for me!!!*"

☞ Mr. Gladstone endeavoured to influence the policy of the Government on the Eastern Question by appealing to the public through the press and on the platform in the cause of the suffering Bulgarians.—1876.

"NO MISTAKE!"

THE BRITISH LION. "*Look here! I don't understand you!—but it's right you should understand me! I DON'T FIGHT, TO UPHOLD WHAT'S GOING ON YONDER!!*"

☞ The misdeeds of the Turkish soldiery in Bulgaria alienated, from all but a few, the sympathies of the country, and tied the hands of the Government.—1876.

"WOODMAN, SPARE THAT TREE!"

Lord Beaconsfield sing—
{ "Woodman, spare that tree! | The Asian Mystère,
I lost it, curse though; | That it has bred till now!"

☞ Mr. Gladstone failed to obtain the support of Parliament to his Resolution condemnatory of the Turkish Government, and was beaten by a majority of 131.—1877.

No. 92.

BENJAMIN BOMBASTES.

"Who dares this pair of Boots displace,
Must meet Bombastes face to face!—
Thus do I challenge all the human race!"

☞ The Ministry addressed a despatch to the Russian Government defining what were British interests, and intimating that if these were endangered they could not hold to their attitude of neutrality.—1877.

No. 93.

ON THE DIZZY BRINK.

LORD B. *"Just a leetle nearer the edge?"*
BRITANNIA. *"Not an inch further. I'm a good deal nearer than is pleasant already!"*

☞ By the despatch of the British Fleet to Constantinople, the risk of a collision with the Russian Forces, resulting in war, was made probable.—1878.

No. 94.

"THE MYSTERIOUS CABINET TRICK."

(Beats MASKELYNE AND COOKE *hollow!)*

☞ Rumours of dissensions in the Cabinet on the question of Peace or War, though denied by Ministers, were acknowledged by the actual resignation of Lord Carnarvon and the threatened resignation of Lord Derby.—1878.
No. 95.

"THE CONFIDENCE TRICK!"

St—ff—rd N—rthc—te (loq.). " *You hand us over your Six Millions—we put it up safe for you, and let you have it again, of course—just to show your* Confidence in us, *don'tyerknow ! ! !*"

☞ The Government asked for a credit of £6,000,000, to strengthen their hands at the approaching Conference, and to show to the European Powers that they possessed the confidence of the country.—1878.

No. 96.

TWO PERSUASIONS.

Mr. Bright made a powerful speech at Manchester disavowing confidence in the Prime Minister, notwithstanding the peaceful professions of the Government.—1878.

No. 97.

OUR "IMPERIAL" GUARD.

LORD B. *"You have often helped HER, Madam."*   INDIA. *"And now I am come to help YOU!"*

[BRITANNIA doesn't exactly know how she likes it.

☞ Lord Beaconsfield electrified the country by the sudden summoning of a body of Indian troops to Malta for service in Europe.—1878.

No. 98.

FIGURES FROM A "TRIUMPH."

(A Relief.—on the Road to Berlin.)

☞ Lord Beaconsfield and the Marquis of Salisbury were appointed Plenipotentiaries to represent the country at the Congress of Berlin.—1878.

"FAÇON DE PARLER!"

LORD B. (opens door, stops suddenly, and whispers). *"Oh, I say! By the bye! What's the French for 'COMPROMISE'"?*

☞ Mr. Punch's assumption that the demands of the Plenipotentiaries would end in a "compromise" was amply proved by the result.—1878.

No. 100.

A "HAPPY FAMILY" AT BERLIN.

SHOWMAN. "*The British Lion and the Roosian Bear will now embrace!* (Aside) *It's all right, ladies and gentlemen, this affair has been* WELL REHEARSED!"

The disclosure of a secret agreement entered into with the Russian Government prior to the assembling of Congress proved that the procedure had been, to some extent, arranged.—1878.

THE SCHOOLMASTER ABROAD.

Bizzy. *"I fancy our friend the Turk don't half like it!"* Duzzy. *"Ha! That's another 'Party' that will have to be 'EDUCATED'"!!*

☞ Mr. Punch here makes allusion to the phrase used by Mr. Disraeli at Edinburgh, in October, 1867. (See Cartoon No. 58.)

No. 102.

A BLAZE OF TRIUMPH!

By the Anglo-Turkish Convention, the British Government contracted to defend the Empire of the Turks in Asia; conditionally upon the adoption of a reformed Administration and the cession of the Island of Cyprus,—which is now garrisoned by British Forces.—1878.

THE "PAS DE DEUX!"

(From the "Scène de Triomphe" in the Grand Anglo-Turkish BALLET D'ACTION.)

☞ Lords Beaconsfield and Salisbury, in reward for their labours as Plenipotentiaries at the Congress, were installed as Knights of the Most Noble Order of the Garter.—1878.

No. 104.